TRANSFORMERS

THE FANTASY, THE FUN, THE FUTURE.

WRITTEN BY
ERIN BRERETON

TRIUMPH
BOOKS

contents

TWO MIGHTY FORCES, LOCKED IN A
CENTURIES-OLD BATTLE FOR RESOURCES,
FOR PLANETS, FOR THE VICTORY
OF GOOD OVER EVIL.

IT'S A STORY OF MACHINES VS. MACHINES,
AND NO MATTER WHAT FORM THEY TAKE —
AS ANIMALS (BEAST WARS AND MACHINES),
AS VEHICLES (AUTOBOT AND DECEPTICON CARS
AND PLANES), AS FAMILIAR MACHINES
(TRANSFORMER ALTERNATORS) — THEY ARE
LOCKED IN A CONSTANT STRUGGLE.

FROM ACTION FIGURES THAT CONVERTED
FROM MACHINE TO ROBOT, TO SUCCESSFUL
TV SERIES, TO COMIC BOOKS AND
A NEW MOVIE THAT IS DUE OUT IN 2007,
THE TRANSFORMERS' LINE HAS
BECOME A FRANCHISE. AND IT'S
ONE THAT'S STILL GROWING.

WE'LL TAKE A LOOK AT THE NEW MOVIE,
INCLUDING ITS STARS, RUMORED PLOT
AND OTHER DETAILS. WE'LL DISCUSS
HOW TRANSFORMERS STARTED,
HOW THEY'VE EVOLVED, THE DIFFERENT
LINES AND SPIN-OFF CARTOON
AND TV SERIES.

WE'RE GOING TO CYBERTRON AND BACK —
ARE YOU READY?

BUCKLE UP.
IT'S GOING TO BE ONE WILD RIDE.

TRANSFORMER TIMES

BACK FOR ANOTHER YEAR OF MOVIE MAYHEM, YOUR FAVORITE AUTOBOTS AND DECEPTICONS ARE GEARING UP FOR THE SILVER SCREEN!

Class is in session! The human cast of the 2007 Transformers movie is widely known—but their Transformer co-stars? Aside from an online chat, confirmation has been scarce. However, rumor has it the fighting-for-good Autobots and dastardly Decepticons below are on board.

There's more to the machine than meets the eye, and this year's crop of robot/vehicle/militia is ready to wage a war the world has never seen!

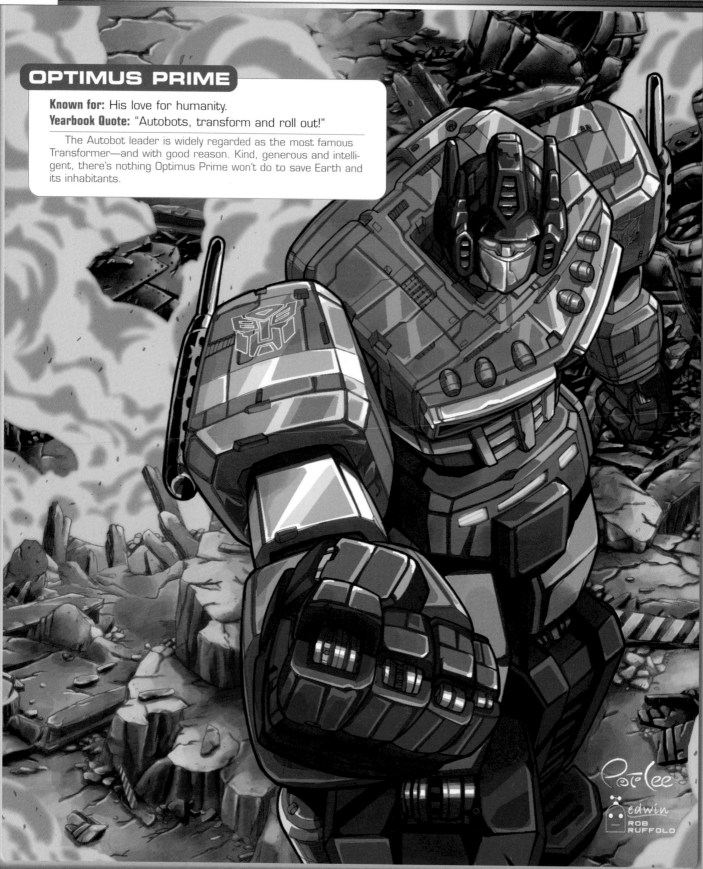

OPTIMUS PRIME

Known for: His love for humanity.

Yearbook Quote: "Autobots, transform and roll out!"

The Autobot leader is widely regarded as the most famous Transformer—and with good reason. Kind, generous and intelligent, there's nothing Optimus Prime won't do to save Earth and its inhabitants.

BUMBLEBEE

Known for: Being an underdog, loving humans, trying to impress.
Yearbook Quote: "Size doesn't matter!"

On the first two seasons of the Transformers TV show (1984-84), Bumblebee and Spike had numerous adventures that took him back to Cybertron, to prehistoric Dinobot Island and other locales. Fans found he was hard to brainwash (leaving it up to him to save his friends from the tricky Decepticons), eager to please and always ready to reach out to humans.

In the first Transformers movie, Bumblebee and his cohort Spike were eaten by Unicorn while still in a ship, but were saved by Spike's son, Daniel. This time around, he'll be the top Autobot scout!

GO-GO GADGETS
HOW THE TOYS HAVE BEEN INSPIRED BY ACTUAL PRODUCTS.

Look—it's a bird! It's a plane! It's … your dad's pick up?

The Transformers were known for their unique design, but in some cases, they were more closely based on p re-existing vehicles than you might have guessed.

Many view the Transformer Alternator line as the most closely based—in part because the Alternators are authentic, licensed 1:24 scale versions of real vehicles. That includes adjustable seats, authentic tires, detailed interiors—just like the real cars (with detachable weapons).

Take, for example, Optimus Prime: Originally, a 1980s semi; in the Alternator line, he's the lost twin to a Dodge Ram SRT-10 pick-up truck, right down to the flip-down tailgate, dash controls and side-view mirrors.

From the Honda Civic to the Ford Mustang, Alternators offer fully poseable robot versions of some of today's hottest cars.

IRON HIDE

Known for: Quick to fight, Mr. Tough Guy
Yearbook Quote: "Optimus and I go way back!"

Heroes fall hard—and such was Ironside's fate in the first film. Will he survive round two with Megatron in the new Transformers movie?

JAZZ

Known for: Sense of style
Yearbook Quote: "Stay cool and look cool."

He's head of operations but often gives the most dangerous assignments to himself—and that, more than anything, describes Jazz's cool, calm and collected manner. He's able to blend in most situations and never gives up.

"I BROUGHT THE BAND-AIDS."

RATCHET

Known for: Expertise in medicine and science
Yearbook Quote: "I brought the band-aids."

Every army needs a medic—and lucky for the Transformers, Ratchet fits the bill. Transforming in the original series into an ambulance, Ratchet is known for his courage and his loyalty.

MEGATRON

Known for: His love of Darwinism and competition; his hatred of humans.

Yearbook Quote: "Show no mercy!"

One of the world's best known villains—and with the ability in different versions to morph into a gun and a tank, it's no stretch of the imagination why. Strong, ruthless, with a love for fighting, Megatron has been known to fire electrical blasts from his hands and laser blasts from his eyes.

He can change size, remains rational in battle, is determined to win. And with little to no known weaknesses, he's sure to give the Autobots a run for their money in the new movie!

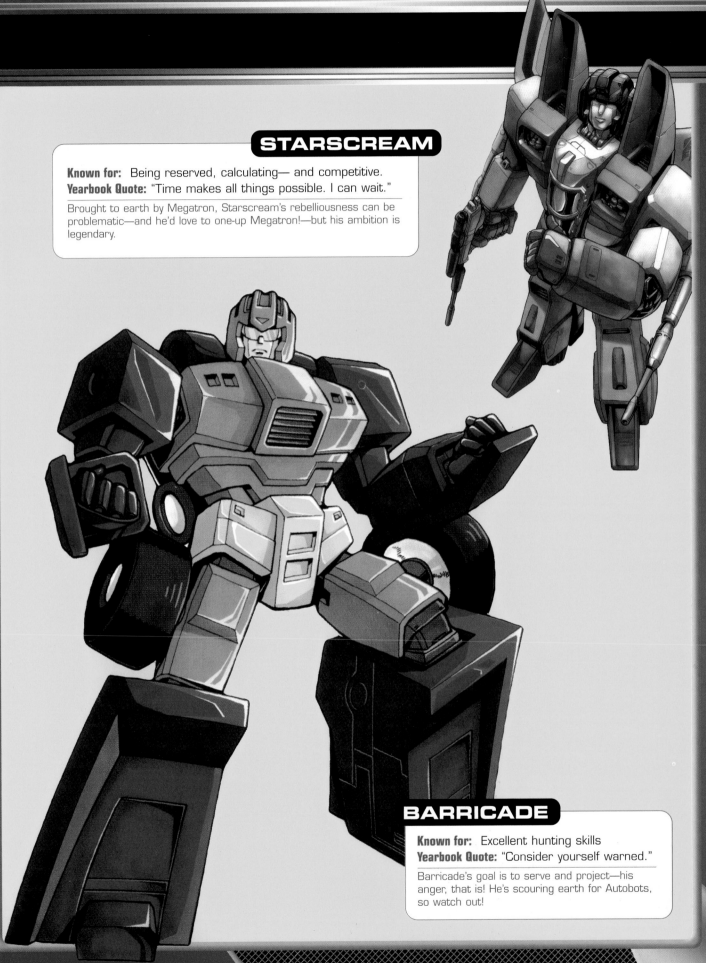

STARSCREAM

Known for: Being reserved, calculating— and competitive.
Yearbook Quote: "Time makes all things possible. I can wait."

Brought to earth by Megatron, Starscream's rebelliousness can be problematic—and he'd love to one-up Megatron!—but his ambition is legendary.

BARRICADE

Known for: Excellent hunting skills
Yearbook Quote: "Consider yourself warned."

Barricade's goal is to serve and project—his anger, that is! He's scouring earth for Autobots, so watch out!

FRENZY

Known for: Small size, spying ability
Yearbook Quote: "I'm watching you!"

Frenzy is ready to rock out—and he's using his small stature to go deep undercover!

BONECRUSHER

Known for: Inability to get along with others—unless you're talking Megatron!
Yearbook Quote: "As you wish, master."

Bonecrusher is bold in battle—but he is boldest when following Megatron's orders. Known to be subservient, Bonecrusher is similar in design to a Constructicon.

BLACKOUT

Known for: Strength in battle, massive size.
Yearbook Quote: "Now hear this..."

Guard your iPod! Blackout can destroy electronic equipment—and he's ready to cripple the Autobot army!

BRAWL

Known for: Always ready to fight!
Yearbook Quote: "You lookin' at me?"

Brawl isn't just fierce—he's strong. Known for his heavy-lifting abilities, he's one Decepticon you don't want to mess with.

SCORPONOK

Known for: Ability to blend into his environment
Yearbook Quote: "Get out of my way—or feel my sting!"

Relenting, ruthless and deadly, no one is safe from Scorponok—after all, he's part robot, part animal, and all mean machine!

13

TRANSFORMER CLASSICS

IT'S A BLAST FROM THE PAST—FIRST GENERATION TRANSFORMERS, ON OVERDRIVE!

Ask almost any collector, and they're sure to list the first generation of Transformers—G1—as a favorite (if not the favorite) of all the Transformer lines.

And with so many variations and more than 20 years of styles, that's not exactly an easy decision to make. But when it comes to Transformers, old school is where it's at! Collectors for years have painstakingly built G1 collections; they've obsessed over storylines that stem from that early era.

And when the new Transformers movie was announced, collectors were hoping G1 bots would be in the cast. It seems like the movie's producers had the same thought: G1 faves like Bumblebee, Optimus Prime, Jazz and other Autobots are rumored to be in the film. G1 Decepticons are also said to be on board, with characters like Megatron and Starscream said to be in the cast.

But the G1 fun is far from over. Hasbro announced plans to produce a Transformer Classics line, based on the old favorites, in summer.

And fans couldn't be more excited.

"This line takes the character designs of the original Generation 1 Transformers and upgrades them with the miracles of modern toy technology," according to the reviewer at forevergeek.com. "The characters have never looked so good."

A review on popular fan site Ben's World of Transformers (www.bwtf.com) echoes the fan's happiness over the Classics line new take on old favorites: "Transformers Classics returns to the basics of the original Transformers by resurrecting several Generation One characters with forms true to their original 80's counterparts utilizing today's toy design techniques. The result [is] Transformers that are both familiar and fresh at the same time."

WHO IS TAKARA?

Founded in 1995, Takara is a Japanese toy company known for creating the Transformers (back before they were called Transformers) and Battle Beasts (which were called BeastFormers in Japan). Takara is located in Toyko.

Takara and Hasbro's partnership is so strong that they are both involved with the upcoming Transformers movie.

"The Transformers brand has always struck a chord with fans around the world and remains one of our strongest franchises since it was introduced 20 years ago," said Keita Satoh, president and chief executive officer of Takara. "Together with Hasbro, DreamWorks and Paramount, we will bring the property to a new level for fans in the Japanese market, as well as around the world."

Hasbro agrees.

"We are truly fortunate to have the best talent in the entertainment industry on board for the Transformers movie and are excited at the opportunities this powerful collaboration will bring to the property," said Brian Goldner, President of Hasbro's toys segment. "The Transformers franchise has been successful in many entertainment arenas and we are thrilled to give millions of fans an extraordinary experience that's never been done in the history of the brand."

WHAT'S NEW?

According to Hasbro, the figures will have more detailed faces and bodies, making them look more like the characters seen on the original TV show and animated movie.

2006

TRANSFORMERS

BOTCON

GENERATIONS

In late September 2006, collectors gathered at BotCon 2006 received an early glimpse at the Transformer Classics being released in October.

Unveiled at the Transformers Product Panel portion of BotCon, the line was introduced by designer Aaron Archer, who walked attendees through the Classic Deluxe, Legends, Voyager and Classic Mini-Con 3-pack releases.

They were an almost immediate hit: And to anyone who knew Transformers, this wasn't a surprise.

Even Hasbro seemed certain the Classics line would be a success. Just look at the enthusiastic message from a Hasbro press release describing the Classics: "Each classics item reaches back into **TRANSFORMER** history to celebrate the classic characters and designs that started it all."

DIDYA KNOW?
Takara Toys also made Bowlingual, a device that says it can "translate" a dog's barking into the human language. Seriously!

TEAMBUILDING

HASBRO AND TAKARA TAKE TOYS TO A NEW LEVEL

Japanese toy company Takara's Diaclone and Micro Change toylines were ready for a change when American toy company Hasbro entered the scene in 1984 and suggested changing their name to Transformers.

And a phenomenon was born: Takara created the newly named Transformers and Hasbro sold and promoted them.

NEXT GENERATION

GENERATION 2 TRANSFORMERS (1992-1995)

Use our handy checklist to make sure you've got the entire second generation of Transformers!

1992

AUTOBOT FIGURES

Autobot Cars
- [ ] Jazz
- [ ] Inferno
- [ ] Sideswipe
- [ ] Dinobots
- [ ] Grimlock
- [ ] Slag
- [ ] Snarl

Autobot Leader
- [ ] Optimus Prime with Roller and Combat Deck

DECEPTICON FIGURES

Constructicons (Yellow)
- [ ] Bonecrusher
- [ ] Scavenger
- [ ] Scrapper
- [ ] Hook
- [ ] Long Haul
- [ ] Mixmaster

Decepticon Jets
- [ ] Starscream
- [ ] Ramjet

Constructicons (Orange)
- [ ] Bonecrusher
- [ ] Scavenger
- [ ] Scrapper
- [ ] Hook
- [ ] Long Haul
- [ ] Mixmaster

1993

AUTOBOT FIGURES

Dinobots
- [ ] Grimlock (Turquoise)
- [ ] Grimlock (Dark Blue)
- [ ] Slag (Red)

- [ ] Slag (Green)
- [ ] Snarl (Red)
- [ ] Snarl (Green)

Mini-Vehicles
- [ ] Beachcomber
- [ ] Bumblebee
- [ ] Hubcap
- [ ] Seaspray

Autobot Cars
- [ ] Rapido
- [ ] Skram
- [ ] Turbofire
- [ ] Windbreaker

Color Changing Cars
- [ ] Drench

Gobots

DECEPTICON FIGURES

Small Jets
- [ ] Afterburner
- [ ] Eagle Eye
- [ ] Terradive
- [ ] Windrazor

Color Changing Cars
- [ ] Deluge
- [ ] Jetstorm

Decepticon Leader
- [ ] Megatron

1994

AUTOBOT FIGURES

Aerialbots
- [ ] Air Raid
- [ ] Fireflight
- [ ] Skydive
- [ ] Slingshot
- [ ] Silverbolt

Rotor Force Autobots
- [ ] Manta Ray

- [ ] Leadfoot

Laser Rod Autobots
- [ ] Electro
- [ ] Volt

Autobot Hero
- [ ] Optimus Prime

DECEPTICON FIGURES

Combaticons
- [ ] Blast Off
- [ ] Brawl
- [ ] Swindle
- [ ] Vortex
- [ ] Onslaught

Rotor Force Decepticons
- [ ] Powerdive
- [ ] Ransack
- [ ] Laser Rods
- [ ] Sizzle
- [ ] Jolt

Decepticon Hero
- [ ] Megatron

Decepticon ATB Stealth Assault Vehicle
- [ ] Dreadwing with Smokescreen

EXCLUSIVES

BotCon
- [ ] Breakdown

1995

AUTOBOT FIGURES

Laser Cycle
- [ ] Road Rocket

Cyberjets
- [ ] Air Raid
- [ ] Jetfire
- [ ] Strafe

Go-Bots
- [ ] Blowout
- [ ] Gearhead
- [ ] Firecracker
- [ ] Motormouth
- [ ] Double Clutch
- [ ] High Beam
- [ ] Optimus Prime
- [ ] Sideswipe
- [ ] Bumblebee
- [ ] Mirage
- [ ] Ironhide

Autobot Leader
- [ ] Laser Optimus Prime

DECEPTICON FIGURES

Laser Cycle
- [ ] Road Pig
- [ ] Auto Rollers
- [ ] Dirtbag
- [ ] Roadblock
- [ ] Cyberjets
- [ ] Skyjack
- [ ] Hooligan
- [ ] Space Case

Go-Bots
- [ ] Megatron
- [ ] Soundwave
- [ ] Frenzy

EXCLUSIVES

BotCon
- [ ] Nightracer

THIS JUST IN!

Hasbro announced the following Classics at the 2006 BotCon Convention:
- [ ] Jetfire
- [ ] Mirage
- [ ] Grimlock
- [ ] Cliffjumper
- [ ] Ramjet

CALL OF THE WILD: BEAST MACHINES

Made for the Millennium, Beast Machines were the next stage of Beast Wars. The Maximal robots returned to Cybertron but were instantly attacked by Vehicons, Megatron's army of vehicles. (Which were also, of course, released as collectible toys).

The Maximals' planet was enslaved, but they kept fighting—and to help, Hasbro released a new line, Beast Machines Battle for the Spark. These action features were activated by pressing a spark crystal.

23

BUMBLEBEE

Yellow and fast, this small sports car isn't quite what it first appears to be, which helps Bumblebee get in and out of tight squeezes and take risks the larger Transformers can't take!

TRICKSTERS: DECEPTICONS

Every army has its tricks—but the Decepticons seem to have an unlimited amount! These dastardly devils can be sneaky, underhanded and—well, just plan deceptive!

Their enemy: The Autobots. Their motive: To control the galaxy, starting with earth, which is desired because of its energy resources.

Yet the Decepticons don't even always trust each other. (Anyone remember Starscream's attempt to overthrow a weakened Megatron in 2005?) You can count on them for in-fighting, personal goals and a general sense of evil—we'd expect nothing less!

CAGE MATCH

WHO LET THE BEASTS OUT? AND AGAINST THE G1 TRANSFORMERS, WHO WOULD WIN?

What if the Generation 1 Transformers faced off against their ancient Beast Wars counterparts? The battle would be fierce, that's for sure. We've picked a group of our favorites from the different years of production and we're calling our bets!

GOOD

Beast Wars Maximal Advantages:
The Beast Wars Maximal/Autobot team is strong. Rattrap is good with all kinds of weaponry, especially explosives, but he is sneaky by nature and would rather go on a Predacon information raid. Cheetor is fast—and quick to strike. He is, however, young and impulsive.

Also known for his demolition skills (note he is sporting a missile), Bonecrusher is a fighting machine, and in battle, seems almost unstoppable!

The G1 Autobot Counterparts:
Every army needs a medic, and Ratchet fits the bill for Generation 1! As a result, he's not as into battle as the other G1s, but he's been known to fight! Jazz is Mr. Cool, and although he's often in charge of planning and executing missions, he isn't afraid to get his hands dirty! Quiet and loyal, Prowl ensures missions go smoothly—which makes him a huge help in battle!

Beast Wars Warriors:
Maximals
Rattrap
Cheetor
Bonecrusher

G1 Transformers
Autobots
Jazz
Prowl
Ratchet

MAXIMALS AND PREDICONS

Maximals, in "Beast Wars," are the peaceful future descendants of the Autobots. They were created after trekking to planet Energois (in reality, Prehistoric Earth), which they needed to do in order to survive the Energon-filled environment. The Autobot-descendants morphed with some of the planet's indigenous animals into these protective, alternative beast modes. The Maximals control Cybertron. Predacons are the descendants of the Decepticons. Both groups are in a very tense truce at the series' start.

PROBABLY EVIL

Beast Wars Predacon Advantages:

The Predacon team is nothing to laugh at, however. Blackarachnia, a former Maximal, knows the Maximal strengths and weaknesses. Rampage's mighty tank-like power can be a physical threat—but the former Maximal is unstable and sadistic. And Razorclaw is an undetectable underwater attacker. If threats come from land or by sea, they're covered!

G1 Decepticon Advantages:

But don't discount the Decepticons. Skywarp is often said to be one of the most sneaky and cunning Decepticons, making him a real threat. Starscream is the Decepticon's fastest flyer—but he can also be gun shy about taking risks. Thundercracker, on the other hand, is also airborn but is a daredevil!

Beast Wars Warriors:

Predacons

Blackarachnia

Rampage

Razorclaw

G1 Transformers

Decepticons

Skywarp

Starscream

Thundercracker

THE WINNER?

Beast Wars and Autobots, without a doubt! They have strategic planning, thanks to Jazz, solid follow-through thanks to Prowl, plus solid fighters Cheetor, who could use Jazz and Prowl's guidance, and Bonecrusher. And, should anyone get hurt, medical help from Ratchet!

The Predacon/Decepticon team, however, isn't so strong. Yes, they've covered both air and sea, but their land resources are weak—and with Rampage's unstable emotional state and Starscream's hesitation in battle, they're likely to be overcome. And who knows where Blackarachnia's loyalties lie? She's been back and forth between both sides—and can't be trusted completely!

DIDYA KNOW?

Bob Forward, one of the "Beast Wars" story editors and writers, also penned several episodes of "The X-Files" and previously wrote for "The Super Mario Bros. Super Show!"

The Production Designer for the "Beast Wars" show, Clyde Klotz, won an Emmy for Outstanding Individual Achievement in Animation in 1997 for his work on Beast Wars, making the series an Emmy award winning show. Klotz is also known for having married Gillian Anderson, aka Scully on "The X-Files." They are divorced but have a daughter, Piper Maru.

WHO ARE THE BEASTS?

First, there were the Beast Wars, a Hasbro-produced toyline made from 1995 to 1999. The Beast Wars figures also had an accompanying TV show, "Beast Wars: Transformers," set in the original Transformers universe, which debuted in 1996 and ran until 1999. All three seasons of the show are available on DVD in the U.S. from Rhino Entertainment, and the first two seasons are currently available in Australia.

Beast Wars was followed up by a new cartoon series, "Beast Machines: Transformers." Fans initially weren't thrilled about the show, which ran from 1999-2001. Their dislike was often attributed to the show's depiction of the surviving Maximals and Predacons acting differently than before, plus structural changes to the planet Cybertron, which had previously been said to have no organic life. In addition, almost none of the writers from "Beast Wars" worked on this second show. But many fans have come to embrace "Beast Machines: Transformers" after its demise.

THEIR

WAR.

OUR

WORLD.

TRANSFORMERS

JULY . 4 . 2007

LIGHTS, CAMERA, LOTS OF ACTION

WE'VE GOT THE SCOOPAGE, PLOT AND MORE EXCITING GOODS ON THE UPCOMING TRANSFORMERS MOVIE!

The Autobots and Decepticons are back—and they're fighting for Earth's future, sometime around July 4, 2007.

That's when the new Transformers film is set to be released—and with a crew of stars already signed on and frequent fan sightings of outdoor filming in cities such as Detroit and LA, it's sure to be a wild ride!

Security and details on the film have been sparse, but fans can't stop talking about what might be going on. One thing remains clear—the people involved with the Transformers movie want to do it right.

"You want to create a pop film but not sell out," star Shia LeBeouf, who plays one of the human cast members, told MTV. "This is a popular film with a following." That's one thing no one is debating!

THE CAST

THE 2007 TRANSFORMERS MOVIE ALSO FEATURES A NUMBER OF HUMAN STARS. THE CELEB LIST IS SAID TO INCLUDE:

JOHN TURTURRO

Respected independent film actor John Turturro plays Agent Simmons in the Transformers movie, but he's also known for his parts in "Anger Management," "Mr. Deeds" and several Spike Lee movies.

SHIA LABEOUF

Shia LaBeouf, who also starred in "The Battle of Shaker Heights" and "Holes," plays Sam Witwicky, who is the 18-year-old human who sets the plot in motion when he tries to sell a pair of his grandfather's old glasses (which are laser-etched with a map and information about the Energon cube) on eBay.

"I play Sam Witwicky, a.k.a. Spike," LaBeouf told MTV. "He's the liaison between the government and the robots, because it's too outlandish for the government to cling onto this idea of this alien [invasion], and they're too close-minded to latch onto it, so they use me as a liaison between the idea of what these things could be and what they actually are."

ANTHONY ANDERSON

Funnyman Anthony Anderson plays Glen in the Transformers movie — and although he's known for playing zany parts in movies such as "Barbershop" and "Scary Movie 4," he also starred in "Hustle and Flow."

MICHAEL O'NEILL

He played a secret service agent on "The West Wing," a Congressman on "Commander In Chief" and now, actor Michael O'Neill is playing a character named Banachek in the new Transformers film. Little is known about the size of his role—but he's sure to be an asset to the cast!

TYRESE GIBSON

Hunky former male model and singer Tyrese Gibson plays USAF Master Sgt. Epps, said to be the leader of one of the military crews in the Transformers movie. Tyrese, as he's known, starred in "Four Brothers," "2 Fast, 2 Furious" and "Baby Boy."

For Gibson, who loved Transformers as a child, the movie was a career turning point, according to MovieWeb. "Everybody else in the film had to audition, and they came at me about the role," Gibson told the press. "I definitely felt fortunate because at this point, no one is able to say that, 'He's only doing films because he can sing.' I got over that bridge that a lot of entertainers, who make a transition, can't get past."

JOSH DUHAMEL

Captain Lennox is played by Josh Duhamel, best known for his role in the "Las Vegas" TV series and "Win a Date with Tad Hamilton!"— and for dating singer Fergie of the Black Eyed Peas.

Not much is known about Captain Lennox, but he is rumored to be leading one of the military crews in the film.

JON VOIGHT

Jon Voight, who plays Keller, has had a long and successful movie career, starring in films like "Lara Croft: Tomb Raider," "Coming Home" and "National Treasure."

MEGAN FOX

Megan Fox's character, Mikaela, is Sam's love interest. "My character is dating the jock, and there's a fight between [Sam and the jock] because I'm stuck in the middle," Fox told MTV. "Each of them has an interest in me. [Sam] ends up helping me out in a specific situation, and through his personality, I start to fall for him. I get caught in the middle of this chase, and that's how I get dragged along and become a part of the rest of the film, with the interaction with the robots."

Fox also appeared in "Confessions of a Teenage Drama Queen" and "Hope and Faith."

RACHAEL TAYLOR

Rachael Taylor, who plays Maggie in the Transformers film, previously appeared in "See No Evil" and the show "McLeod's Daughters." She was born in Australia.

THE PLOT:

The rumored plot is as follows: Fuel supplies on Cybertron, the planet where the good Autobots and evil Decepticons live, are running low, so both robot forces head to Earth in search of energy resources. The good news is Earth has plenty of minerals and chemicals; the bad news is, disguising themselves as planes, boats, cars and more, the Autobots, led by Optimus Prime, and Decepticons, led by Megatron, then battle to determine who will control these resources—and the planet itself.

The screenwriters told fans on a Yahoo! Movies online chat that the Generation 1 cartoon was much more of an influence on the movie than the toys themselves. They have also said, in response to fan concerns that the movie would be too human-intensive, that the screen time of Transformers to humans is about 50/50.

"I only wanted to do Transformers if I could do it realistic," Bay said in an interview. "And from what I've seen and what we've done with our digital studies, putting it in real-world stuff, that is lots of effects around that are real effects, that's how we make it realistic."

DIDYA KNOW?

The movie has been in production for years and at one time was rumored to be set for a 2005 release—which would have been ironic because the 1986 film took place in 2005!

According to the Sci Fi Wire, the film is asking to be the first production to film the exterior of the Pentagon since 9/11.

MAIN VOICES

Details on what actors are voicing the various Autobots and Decepticons has been scarce—in fact, Sci Fi Wire reported that cast and crew members told the news service that voice casting was being delayed until much later in the production.

Although many of the actors who voiced characters in the original 1986 film have since passed away, one key star is said to be returning: Peter Cullen as Optimus Prime!

Cullen is no stranger to voices: He also voiced the role of Eeyore in "Pooh's Heffalump Movie," "The Tigger Movie" and "Piglet's Big Movie."

Frank Welker, who voiced Megatron in the original film, is widely thought to be reprising his role—but that's unconfirmed!

Photo by Wireimage

CHARACTERS

Although unconfirmed outside of an online chat with the movie's screenwriters on Yahoo! Movies, the Transformers said to be in the film are as follows:

AUTOBOTS
Optimus Prime
Bumblebee
Jazz
Ratchet
Ironhide

DECEPTICONS
Megatron
Starscream
Brawl
Bonecrusher
Barricade
Frenzy
Blackout
Scorponok

Why are there more Decepitcons?

Don't discount the underdog! In their Yahoo! Chat, the film's writers said that the numbers were purposefully offset in order to make for better battle scenes because the Autobots are at a disadvantage and must join together to win.

GUEST LIST

Recent reports about the movie have also suggested another surprise: celeb cameos!

Two of the stars making brief appearances in the film include Bernie Mac and Dane Cook. Bernie Mac's character is Bobby Bolivia, according to IMDB.com. One rumor has it that Bernie Mac plays the car dealer who Shia LaBeouf buys his first car from—which is a Transformer in disguise!

Comedian Dane Cook, said to be a lifelong Transformers fanatic, helped create his cameo.

FILMING LOCATIONS FOR THE MOVIE

- The new Transformers movie will film in various cities, such as Los Angeles, CA; Chicago, IL; Detroit, MI and Washington, D.C.

- Backlot, Universal Studios, Universal City, California

- Edwards Air Force Base, California

- Holloman Air Force Base, Alamogordo, New Mexico

- Hoover Dam, Arizona-Nevada Border

- Kirtland Field, Albuquerque, New Mexico

- Rialto, California, USA (State Route 210 Freeway)

- Valley of Fire State Park - Route 169, Overton, Nevada

- White Sands Missile Range, near, Alamogordo, New Mexico

As reported by IMDB.com and other sources.

SCREEN SHOT:
THE FIRST ANIMATED MOVIE

This isn't the Autobots and Decepitcons' first time on the silver screen! The first Transformers movie, "Transformers: The Movie," was released in 1986. Directed by Nelson Shin, who had produced the original Transformer TV show, the movie featured the voices of several big (but older) celebrities—Orson Welles, of "Citizen Kane" fame, Leonard Nimoy from "Star Trek" and Robert Stack, among others.

Based on the TV series, the movie takes place 20 years after the TV series second season. Its tone is darker (Decepticons kill quickly—and often without thought), but several of the TV faves appear—and several beloved characters die.

RUMORED FIGHT SCENE
The writers also alluded to a one-on-one fight between Megatron and Optimus Prime.

CYBERTRON STARS

And here are some live action suggestions for these Cybertron stars:

OPTIMUS PRIME
Role calls for an actor to be: Smart, kind, strong
Perfect Pick: Leonardo DiCaprio
He nailed playing Howard Hughes, who changed the face of flying with his determination!

MEGATRON
Role calls for an actor to be: Cunning, wicked
Perfect Pick: Jack Nicholson
He's scary! Jack's known for playing wicked characters.

BUMBLEBEE
Role calls for an actor to be: Small but mighty
Perfect Pick: Frankie Muniz
According to IMDB.com, this "Malcolm in the Middle" actor is just 5'6"—but he packs a strong acting punch!

STARSCREAM
Role calls for an actor to be: Withdrawn, calculating
Perfect Pick: James Franco
After playing an angry former best friend who wants revenge in "Spider-Man 2," James could perfectly play Starscream's state of mind!

JAZZ
Role calls for an actor to be: Super stylish
Perfect Pick: Sean "Puffy" Combs
Not only is Puff known for his style, he runs a clothing line—and has acted before!

RATCHET
Role calls for an actor to be: Medically-minded
Perfect Pick: Shane West
The former teen idol has was last seen playing a doctor on "ER"!

IRONHIDE
Role calls for an actor to be: Super-tough and ready to fight
Perfect Pick: Michael Chiklis
He's already had a rock hide as the Thing in the "Fantastic Four", why not an iron one? He's too tough to not be a Transformer!

THE ROCK

ROCKINATOR
The Decepticons will smell what The Rock is cooking when they meet up with him in an dark alley! His brute strength allows him to shake, slam and defeat Decepticon forces!

Funny New Characters

NICK LACHEY

ROMANCER

Once married to Jessica Simpson, and now dating MTV VJ Vanessa Minnillo, Nick makes the ladies swoon—and he's using those same powers to dizzy the Autobots during war!

JUSTIN TIMBERLAKE

RAPITRON

He throws down cool beats that heat up Autobot and Decepticon battles by causing earthquake-like destruction with sound waves!

HILLARY DUFF

TEENSAW

Hilary uses her teen fan power to destroy evil forces with a giant lipstick shaped like a chainsaw— it's true, you do have to suffer to be beautiful, when TeenSaw is around!

TIME REMAINING

−278

Days

6:14

Hrs.   Min.

COLLECT THIS

COLLECTORS HAVE HELPED MAKE TRANSFORMERS MORE THAN JUST A PLAYTHING.

Transformers could have just been another toy. Another product with a **TV** series based on it. Another thing boys wanted to play with, for awhile, before it got old.

But the Transformers have survived for more than 20 years—that's no simple plaything.

They have survived—and thrived—because collectors have embraced the toy. Since their release, kids, and some adults, have snatched up every version, launched fan Web sites and attended conventions across the country celebrating the Transformers phenomenon.

2006 TRANSFORMERS BOTCON GENERATIONS

September 29 - October 1, 2006
Lexington, Kentucky

Contains Five TRANSFORMERS Figures with Accessories:

Darksyde Dinobot

Axalon Optimus Primal
Axalon Rhinox
Axalon Cheetor
Axalon Rattrap

TRANSFORMERS TIMELINES

DAWN OF FUTURE'S PAST

Adult Collectible

THE TRANSFORMERS COLLECTORS' CLUB

Membership in the Hasbro's Collector's Club, launched in 2005, includes a monthly subscription to Master Collector, a monthly indexed toy and doll trading newspaper that contains several thousand classified ads. Club members also receive a free 30-word ad each month (which appears in Master Collector and online) so that they can buy, sell and trade Transformer items.

A free Transformer is also part of the membership—the club organizers select one model a year. In 2006, Landquake was the figure.

Every other month, Master Collector has a 16 page, four-color newsletter with information on "everything Transformers, from G1 to Cybertron" stitched inside. Product reviews, new release information, historical articles, shipping schedules and interviews with Transformer designers are also featured.

A 6-page Transformers serial comic is also included in each issue. The story begins with the first issue each year and continues through to the end of the year.

GETTING THE FREE FIGURE

Club members get a free Transformer, but you have to join by March 15 of each year to get it—that's when the free version mails each year! Join after March 15 and you can still buy the figure, but won't receive one until next year.

Memberships are one year, just like the story arc. And back issues of the newsletter are available to members so long as supplies last!

Memberships are $40 or $62, depending on what mail class you select; you can join at 800-772-6673 (toll free).

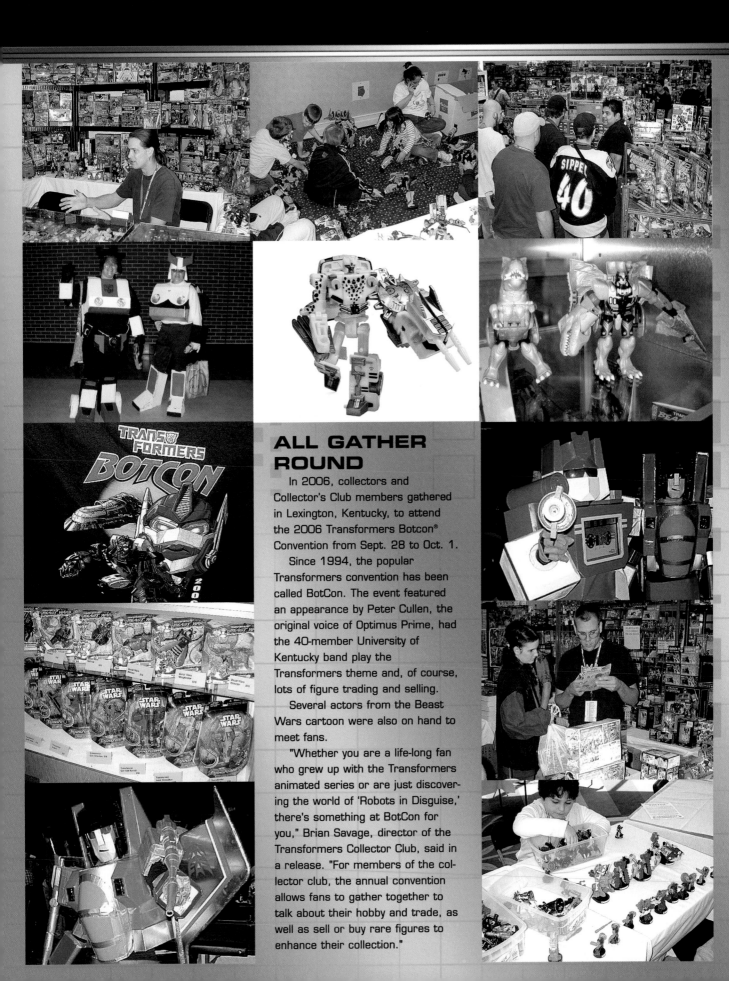

ALL GATHER ROUND

In 2006, collectors and Collector's Club members gathered in Lexington, Kentucky, to attend the 2006 Transformers Botcon® Convention from Sept. 28 to Oct. 1.

Since 1994, the popular Transformers convention has been called BotCon. The event featured an appearance by Peter Cullen, the original voice of Optimus Prime, had the 40-member University of Kentucky band play the Transformers theme and, of course, lots of figure trading and selling.

Several actors from the Beast Wars cartoon were also on hand to meet fans.

"Whether you are a life-long fan who grew up with the Transformers animated series or are just discovering the world of 'Robots in Disguise,' there's something at BotCon for you," Brian Savage, director of the Transformers Collector Club, said in a release. "For members of the collector club, the annual convention allows fans to gather together to talk about their hobby and trade, as well as sell or buy rare figures to enhance their collection."

FUNNY PAGES

TRANSFORMER COMICS

Transformers comics helped fans get to know characters, battles and much more—and they created a whole new group of Transformer addicts!

Comic fans are known for their dedication. They are completely faithful to certain writers, cartoonists, religiously follow plotlines and snatch up copy after copy.

It's no surprise, then, that Transformer fans would find a comic book series based on their favorite Cybertron residents fascinating. Since their debut in the mid 1980s, Transformer-themed comics have continued to thrive, despite switching publishers, formats and even the characters themselves.

Fans generally attribute three companies with having produced the three largest comic Transformer comic franchises.

WHAT A MARVEL

The first series was made from 1984 to 1991 by Marvel comics and had an 80-issue run. The Marvel comic is often thought to be the most popular.

Marvel also released a 4-series, special edition comic that featured the Transformers alongside another popular toy of the 1980s, such as G.I. Joe. The tough-but-tiny soldier joined the Autobots in their fight against the Decepticons

A second, "Transformers: Generation 2," ran for 12 issues, beginning in 1993. Also produced by Marvel, the fight included the entire galaxy, instead of just Cybertron or Earth. The series ended with a giant battle between the Generation 1 Transformers, the Swarm (based off Generation 2 Decepticons) and Cybertronians, residents of Cybertron.

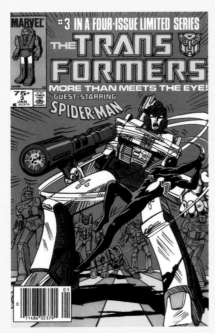

JUST LIKE A DREAM

Dreamwave Productions created another licensed comic series that ran from 2002 to 2004, which included several limited series, featuring Generation 1 Transformers.

Dreamwave's series was based on the current Transformers Armada toyline. Starting out with another writer, respected previous UK-Marvel version writer Simon Furman again came on board to do a 2-part story and ended up staying on to write.

After #18, the issue was retitled "Transformers: Energon" and began taking place 10 years after the Armada series.

Dreamwave also produced a six-issue G.I. Joe and Transformers crossover series. But by issue #30, Dreamwave was having serious financial trouble and the series ended when the company went bankrupt in 2005.

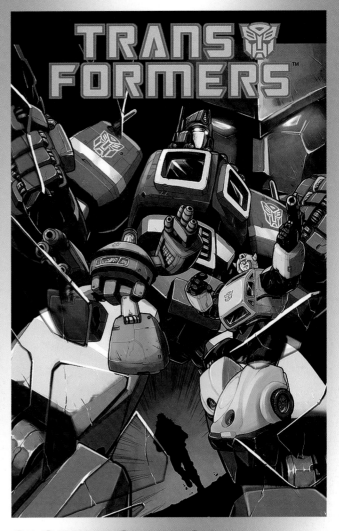

GLOBETROTTING
TRANSFORMER COMICS OUTSIDE THE U.S.

Think the Transformers got around Cybertron more than they traveled around Earth? Think again! A wildly popular UK version of the Transformers comic ran for more than 300 issues. Because the UK version was weekly, the comic, written by Simon Furman, was known for its well-developed characters and plotlines. Since the U.S. version was monthly, and the UK much more frequent, they had to insert their own comics into each issue. It ran from 1984 to 1992.

Japanese comics were also available. The "Transformers: The Comics" manga collection, from Japan, which first debuted in 1985, in the publication "TV Magazine." Based on the animated series, the comics were created in Japan until 1992.

At a recent IDW Panel at the BotCon 2006 convention, the Transformer comic creators revealed that if it makes sense to the story, Japanese G1 characters might appear in future issues.

A NEW ID

IDW Publishing is currently carrying the comic torch. It licensed the Transformers series starting in October 2005 and has been regularly publishing since January 2006. IDW has also produced limited series of the comic.

Originally planned as two miniseries, one about G1 characters and one about the Beast Wars characters, the comics were such a hit, IDW has been able to do other comic projects. They even brought writer Simon Furman back on board.

SOME OF THE COMIC SERIES IDW HAS PRODUCED ARE:

- "The Transformers" Infiltration": Starting in October 2005, this 6-issue series features the Transformers on Earth.
- "The Transformers: Stormbringer": This series features the Transformers, because Cybertron has been destroyed by war, spread out across the universe. First published in July 2006.
- "Beast Wars: The Gathering"—A four-issue series released in 2006, set after season two of the Beast Wars cartoon series, but with some characters not featured in that series.

STORYTIME

TRANSFORMER COMICS ARE KNOWN FOR THEIR POPULAR PLOTS!

SOME FAN FAVORITES INCLUDE:

1st U.S. Marvel Comic: Optimus Prime leads the Autobots against the Decepticons after landing on Earth and lying dormant for 4,000,000 years.

Transformers Dreamwave Armada #17: Concluding the "Worlds Collide" arc, Optimus Prime returns, the time-traveling Decepticons are killed and the Armada land seems to be calm. However, Unicron is also back—which might spell trouble!

GAME ON

HASBRO IS GEARING UP FOR A WHOLE NEW PLAY ON TRANSFORMERS—NEW GAMES, STARTING WITH ONE BASED ON THE UPCOMING MOVIE.

When you're dealing with something as tech-friendly as robots and cars, making the leap to becoming a video game is a no-brainer. At least, it shouldn't be.

However, after several versions of Transformer-based games that didn't quite hit the mark, fans are hoping that the new video game in the works will finally bring the Transformer franchise to where it needs to be—in the hands of Transformer fans. Literally.

In February, Hasbro announced that it had partnered with Activision to create new console, handheld and PC games featuring the Transformers. The first will be based on the upcoming 2007 Transformers movie.

"We are thrilled to work with Activision to bring the widely popular Transformers brand to the world of digital entertainment," Jane Ritson-Parsons, president of the Hasbro Properties Group (HPG), said in a release. "As the leading developer of video games, Activision shares our passion and excitement for the Transformers story line. We know this world-class and creative team will bring Transformers to life in powerful and exciting ways as we immerse a broad audience in this pop-culture phenomenon."

Activision is excited, too. "Transformers have all of the elements necessary to translate incredibly well into video games," said Mike Griffith, president and CEO, Activision Publishing, Inc. "We look forward to bringing the Transformer robots to life with the latest interactive technology and graphics."

Currently being developed, several stills from the game were leaked

CLASSICS

REVIEWS OF EXISTING TRANSFORMER VIDEOGAMES

1985
Ocean Software Version—Not well-received.

1986
Activision Version—Also didn't reach its full potential.
Japanese Version—Not popular; never made it to the U.S.
PlayStation 2 Version—Although reaction was mixed, this game is the most popular to date. But it features no humans. Its graphics were well-received but players criticized its repetitiveness.

PREVIOUS PLAYS

But this new 2007 game won't be the Transformers first appearance on video game consoles across America. In 1985, Ocean Software Ltd. released a video game for ZX Spectrum and Commodore 64.

While not a huge hit with fans, it was successful enough to inspire a 1986 Activision version for the Commodore 64.

In Japan, Takara released a game named Transformers: Convoy no Nazo, which was generally said to be poorly received.

A more popular release was the PlayStation 2 version by Atari. Simply called "Transformers," it is most closely based on the Armada series. Although not a wild hit, reaction was mixed and some collectors liked the game. The player could choose to be Optimus Prime, Red Alert or Hot Shot and could go from vehicle to robot mode on the battlefield—and fight against Megatron!

SiMPLY THE BEST

TAKE A LOOK AT THE TOP 10 GOOD AND BAD TRANSFORMERS!

All-good Autobots. Dastardly Decepticons. Transformers have taken their battle from Cybertron to earth—and beyond.

Battling desperately over earth's energy resources, the two forces are both strong—but one believes in fighting dirty, and the other in fighting fair.

And in this battle, there have been many victors and many heroes—check out this list of the top 10!

LANDQUAKE

Who He Is: He's strong, and he's fierce!

Fans Love Him Because: He was such a fan favorite he was this year's pick for the Transformer Collector's Club free figurine!

OPTIMUS PRIME

Who He Is: Fighter, rational planner and born leader.

Fans Love Him Because: Optimus Prime is set to lead the Autobots to victory—and save Earth in the process!

JAZZ

Who He Is: A mission planner with a serious sense of style.

Fans Love Him Because: Collectors love his charm—and with his superior battle planning skills, Jazz is one Transformer you want on your side!

BUMBLEBEE

Who He Is: Small, eager to please and friendly to humans.

Fans Love Him Because: As a buddy of mankind, Bumblebee is an obviously well-liked Transformer!

IRON HIDE

Who He Is: A tough and quick-to-battle Transformer!

Fans Love Him Because: Not only do fans love this tough Transformer, his history with Optimus Prime makes him a prime candidate for being in the action!

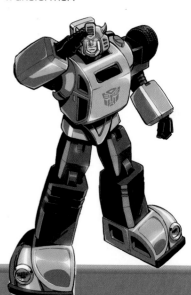

MEGATRON

Who He Is: He's ready to lead the Decepticons in war against the Autobots.

Fans Love Him Because: He's so ruthless, Transformer addicts can't wait to see what his next move will be!

BONECRUSHER

Who He Is: He's hard to get along with but he's a risk taker.

Fans Love Him Because: His risky nature makes Bonecrusher a thrill to watch in battle!

GALVATRON

Who He Is: The 2nd Decepticon leader is essentially a new version of Megatron.

Fans Love Him Because: He may not be Megatron, but he's just as nasty!

STARSCREAM

Who He Is: He's patient and deadly.

Fans Love Him Because: Starscream isn't even afraid of Megatron—and fans aren't afraid to ask for more of Starscream in Transformer plots!

BRAWL

Who He Is: Strong and reactive.

Fans Love Him Because: Transformers enthusiasts love that Brawl is always ready to fight, fierce and super strong

MOVIE REAL

Video games aren't the only products being released to promote the 2007 movie! Although it's too early to know the full extent of what Hasbro has planned, they have announced it plans to release Transformer ring tones, mobile gaming and other products.

AT BOTCON 2006, OTHER NEW MOVIE TIE-INS WERE ANNOUNCED, INCLUDING:

- Two new movie preview figurines, released May 2, 2007 (just about two months before the movie!)
- A full toy line based on the movie characters.
- Alternators will end before the movie, but may come back after!

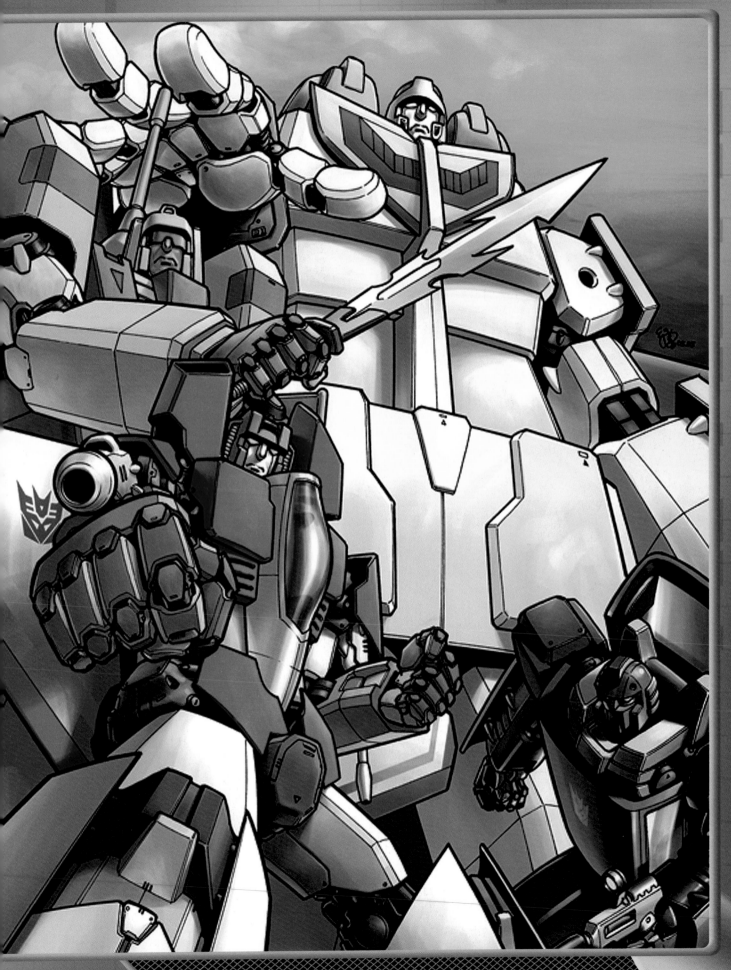

FIGHTING THE GOOD FIGHT.

THAT'S THE AUTOBOTS HAVE BEEN DOING FOR CENTURIES—AND ALTHOUGH WE MAY BE ROOTING FOR THEM, WATCHING THE DECEPTICONS PLOT AND PLOY IS ALMOST AS FUN. BREATHTAKING BATTLES, INSANELY QUICK CONVERSIONS FROM ROBOT TO VEHICLE, SPECIAL SKILLS THAT MAKE EACH ONE UNIQUE—THAT'S JUST PART OF THE TRANSFORMERS EXPERIENCE.

THAT EXPERIENCE IS ABOUT TO GET A WHOLE LOT MORE EXCITING. IN SUMMER 2007, A LIVE-ACTION TRANSFORMERS MOVIE WILL BE RELEASED, FEATURING CELEBRITIES LIKE JOSH DUHAMEL, SHIA LABEOUF, TYRESE GIBSON, DANE COOK AND MORE. NEW FIGURES, BASED ON THE FILM, ARE ALSO SET FOR RELEASE.

AND THE TRANSFORMERS FRANCHISE GROWS. THE SUCCESSFUL LINES LIKE BEAST WARS AND MACHINES, ALTERNATORS AND MORE, REMAIN HIGHLY COLLECTIBLE. THE ORIGINAL 1986 MOVIE IS COMING OUT ON DVD. THE TV SHOWS ARE COLLECTOR'S ITEMS.

AND SOMEWHERE ON EARTH, WHERE YOU LEAST EXPECT IT—MAYBE YOUR TOWN, MAYBE EVEN YOUR STREET—THE TRANSFORMERS ARE WAG-ING A SECRET BATTLE FOR THE VERY PLANET ITSELF. OUR FUTURE—AND THEIRS—HANGS IN THE BALANCE. WILL THE AUTOBOTS DEFEAT THE DECEPTICONS? ONLY TIME WILL TELL.

AND FROM COLLECTING, TO COMICS, TO CONVENTIONS, WE WILL ALL BE ALONG FOR THE RIDE. TRUE TRANSFORMER FANS WOULDN'T HAVE IT ANY OTHER WAY.